Without Wings, Mother, How Can I Fly?

For Micah and Joy —K.N.

Henry Holt and Company, Inc., *Publishers since 1866*
115 West 18th Street, New York, New York 10011

Henry Holt is a registered trademark
of Henry Holt and Company, Inc.
Text copyright © 1998 by Thomas Farber
Illustrations copyright © 1998 by Keiko Narahashi
All rights reserved.
Published in Canada by Fitzhenry & Whiteside Ltd.,
195 Allstate Parkway, Markham, Ontario L3R 4T8.

Library of Congress Cataloging-in-Publication Data
Farber, Norma.
Without wings, mother, how can I fly? / Norma Farber;
illustrations by Keiko Narahashi.
Summary: A mother's responses reassure her child when he wonders
how he can do the many things animals can do without their natural abilities.
[1. Mother and child—Fiction. 2. Animals—Fiction. 3. Stories in rhyme.]
I. Narahashi, Keiko, ill. II. Title. PZ8.3.F224Wi 1997
[E]—dc21   97-12863

ISBN 0-8050-3380-7
First Edition—1998
The artist used watercolor on rag paper to create the illustrations for this book.
Printed in the United States of America on acid-free paper.∞
10 9 8 7 6 5 4 3 2 1

Without Wings, Mother, How Can I Fly?

Norma Farber   illustrated by Keiko Narahashi

Henry Holt and Company • New York

Without wings, Mother,
how can I fly?

In a plane, my dear,
like a bird across the sky.

Without a tail,
      how can I swing in the breeze?

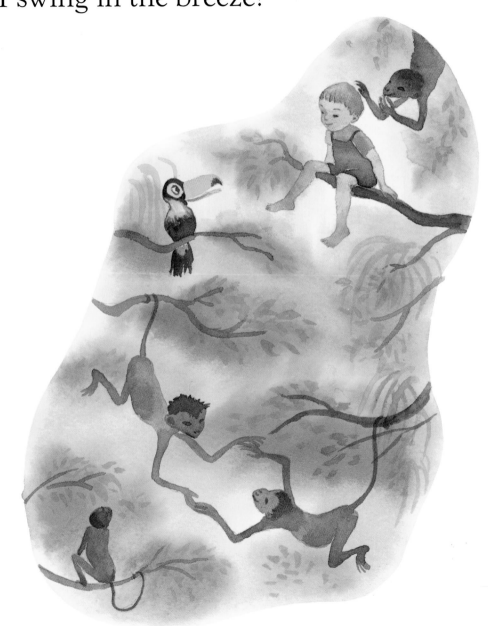

By ropes and a board,
hung from the tallest of trees.

How can I change my skin,
so I won't be seen?

Put another jacket on:
your gray or your green.

How can I spin a web,
   without a spider's thread?

Try catching moths
with a net of gauze, instead.

Spittle-bugs blow bubbles.
  Can I do that?

With suds and a pipe.
Blow slowly; they puff up fat.

Without fins, Mother,
   how can I swim in the pond?

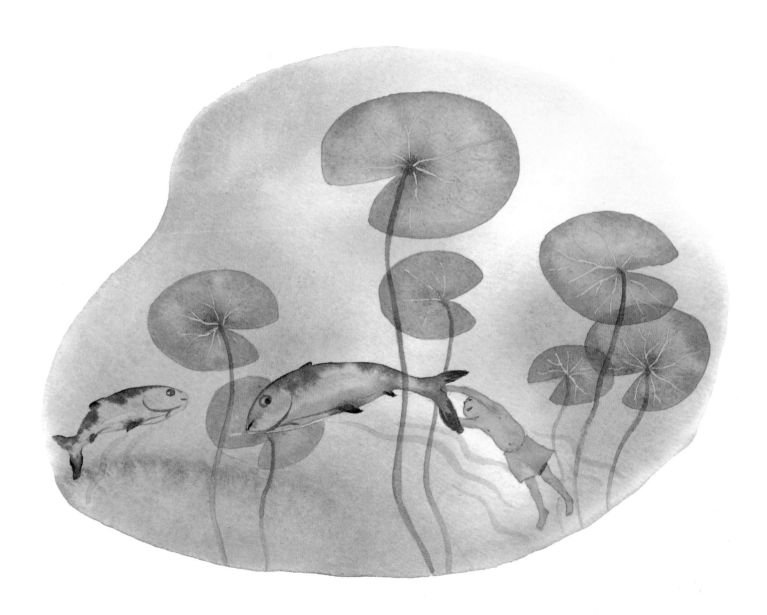

Just kick your legs.
You'll reach the raft, and beyond.

I want to duck underwater,
  and stay awhile.

Just hold your breath.
Take time, like a crocodile.

Without a trunk,
  what can I use for a shower?

Stand under the garden sprinkler,
some sunny hour.

But claws—
I need them to climb for plums and pears.

A ladder will lead you up
by rungs or stairs.

Well, without feelers,
how can I find a treat?

Just come when dinner's ready.
Come and eat!

Without a glowworm's fire,
can I see in the dark?

Oh yes,
your flashlight throws a steady spark.

How to sleep warm?
  I haven't got a furry skin.

You have flannel pajamas,
soft to be cuddled in.

Can I snuggle up tight,
   like a tiny silk cocoon?

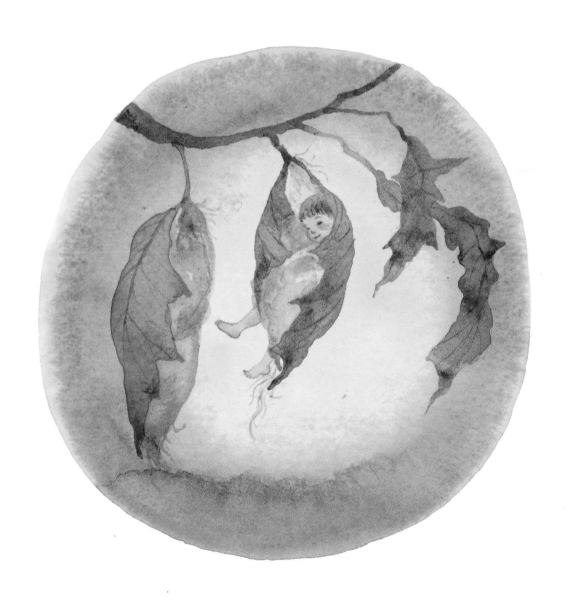

Yes, in a sleeping bag.
It's bedtime soon.

But without a shell,
　　how can I keep from harm?

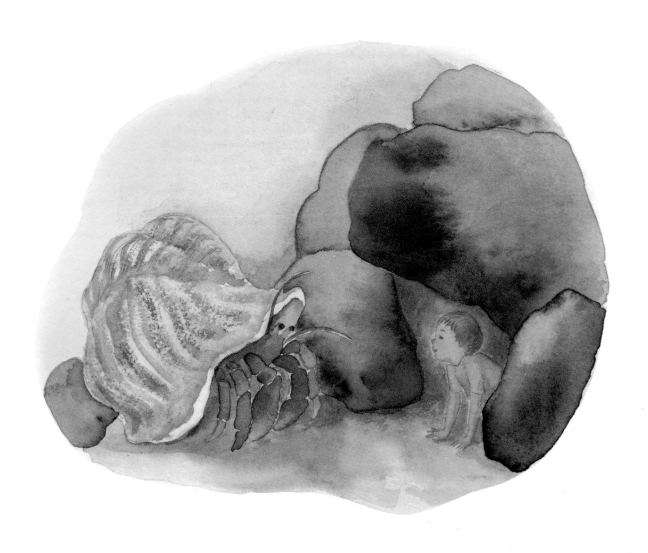

Here, right here,
safe in the curve of my arm.